GROUNDHOG DAY FROM THE BLACK LAGOON®

Get more monster-sized laughs from

The Black Lagoon®

#1: The Class Trip from the Black Lagoon
#2: The Talent Show from the Black Lagoon
#3: The Class Election from the Black Lagoon
#4: The Science Fair from the Black Lagoon
#5: The Halloween Party from the Black Lagoon
#6: The Field Day from the Black Lagoon
#7: The School Carnival from the Black Lagoon
#8: Valentine's Day from the Black Lagoon
#9: The Christmas Party from the Black Lagoon
#10: The Little League Team from the Black Lagoon
#11: The Snow Day from the Black Lagoon
#12: April Fools' Day from the Black Lagoon
#13: Back-to-School Fright from the Black Lagoon
#14: The New Year's Eve Sleepover from the Black Lagoon
#15: The Spring Dance from the Black Lagoon
#16: The Thanksgiving Day from the Black Lagoon
#17: The Summer Vacation from the Black Lagoon
#18: The Author Visit from the Black Lagoon
#19: St. Patrick's Day from the Black Lagoon
#20: The School Play from the Black Lagoon
#21: The 100th Day of School from the Black Lagoon
#22: The Class Picture Day from the Black Lagoon
#23: Earth Day from the Black Lagoon
#24: The Summer Camp from the Black Lagoon
#25: Friday the 13th from the Black Lagoon
#26: The Big Game from the Black Lagoon
#27: The Amusement Park from the Black Lagoon
#28: Secret Santa from the Black Lagoon

GROUNDHOG DAY FROM THE BLACK LAGOON®

by Mike Thaler

Illustrated by Jared Lee

SCHOLASTIC INC.

To Bruce, Diana, and family
—M.T.

To Captain Topper
—J.L.

ISBN 978-0-545-78520-4

12 11 10 9 8 7 6 5 4 16 17 18 19/0

Printed in the U.S.A. 40
First printing, January 2015

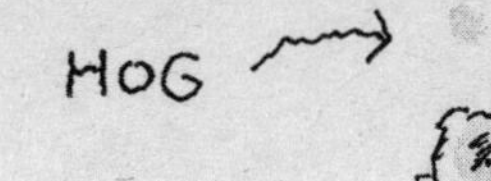

CONTENTS

CHAPTER 1
HUMHOG

Mrs. Green told our class we're going to be doing a morning news show in February. We all got our assignments and, sadly enough for February 2nd, I'm the anchorman. And on top of that, it's Groundhog Day.

OH, GREAT.

There are many silly holidays but the silliest of all has to be *Groundhog Day*. The idea that a large rodent can forecast the weather is ridiculous! Next they will have an *anchor rat* on the morning news.

It was only a week away so I had to research the best I could. I went straight to the library after school.

CHAPTER 2
THE SHADOW KNOWS

Our librarian, Mrs. Beamster, told me "Groundhog Day started on February 2, 1887. The settlers of Punxsutawney, Pennsylvania, had an old legend that if a groundhog sees his shadow in early February there will be six more weeks of winter. It became official and an annual holiday."

MRS.
BEAMSTER
HERE'S A
BOOK ON
SHADOWS.
INTERESTING!

"Silly," I said.

"The folks in Punxsutawney don't feel that way," said Mrs. Beamster.

OH, NO. PAPA, SIX MORE WEEKS OF WINTER.

CHAPTER 3
MAMA KNOWS BEST

When I got home, I told Mom about the holiday.

"Punxsutawney Phil is very famous," said Mom. "His forecast is right 39 percent of the time."

"Anyone can be right 39 percent of the time. Even I'm right 39 percent of the time. They could have picked a turkey, a cow, or an elephant. They have an even bigger shadow."

"That's not the point, Hubie. By tradition, Punxsutawney Phil *is* a groundhog."

"I bet even Tailspin could be right 39 percent of the time."

CHAPTER 4
GOING TO THE DOGS

"I'll prove it," I said. I got a box and took Tailspin out into the backyard.

I put the box on the ground and Tailspin went in. He came right out and licked my face. It was hard getting him back in the box, so after an hour of trying, I gave up on the weather forecast and ran around the yard having a good time.

CHAPTER 5
GROUNDHOG FEVER

At school the next day, everyone made a big deal of the coming holiday. There were drawings of groundhogs all along the hall.

"Humhog," I muttered as I walked to class. All day we did groundhog crossword puzzles, mazes, word scrambles, and connect the groundhog dots.

There was even a Groundhog Day play in the cafeteria. Eric played the lead. He actually looked a little like a groundhog. I just sat in the middle of it all.

Humhog! I thought. *Humhog.*

MAYOR, CAN PHIL THE GROUNDHOG SEE HIS SHADOW?
YES, TOWNSPEOPLE, WE WILL HAVE SIX MORE WEEKS OF WINTER.
SUN
MAYOR
PHIL
BURROW
22

CHAPTER 6
THE GREEN TEAM

After school, Mrs. Green met with the news team. Freddie would report on the cafeteria lunch, Derek would do sports, Penny would do social events, Doris would give the pledge, Eric would ask a riddle, and I would report on the BIG event: the news from Punxsutawney, Pennsylvania.

TASTY FISH STICKS TODAY.
GIRL'S BASKETBALL PRACTICE AFTER SCHOOL.
THE CHESS TOURNAMENT HAS BEEN CANCELLED BECAUSE NOBODY KNOWS HOW TO PLAY IT.
I PLEDGE ALLEGIANCE TO THE FLAG...
WHAT RUNS AROUND THE YARD, BUT NEVER MOVES?
A FENCE.
OH, BROTHER.

CHAPTER 7
HOGZILLA

That night, I had a hogmare. I was reading the news and the weatherman came out, but he wasn't a man—he was a giant groundhog. A *huge* groundhog.

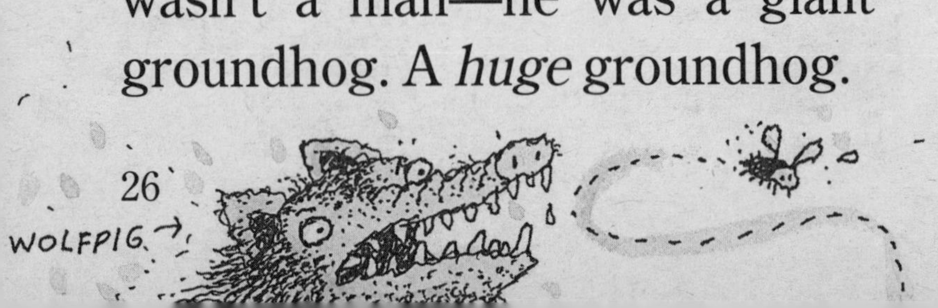

NEWS

In fact . . . he was *Hogzilla.* He cast a *big* shadow. He lumbered through the wall of the library and out into the school yard. He knocked over the jungle gym and the swings. Then he turned and came back into the school and picked me up.

“Well, folks, I guess we’re in for six more weeks of winter,” I said.

CHAPTER 8
FOOD FOR THOUGHT

As the big day finally came closer, the groundhog fever grew.

“I just hope we don’t have groundhog burgers for lunch tomorrow,” I said.

"I wonder what they would taste like?" asked Freddy.

"Probably like chicken," piped up Eric.

"Why chicken?" I asked.

"'Cause everything weird tastes like chicken."

MENU
RACCOON
POSSUM
ARMADILLO
COYOTE
BUZZARD
MONKEY
DONKEY
AND TODAY'S SPECIAL
TARANTULA
IT DOESN'T MATTER WHAT YOU ORDER IT WILL TASTE LIKE CHICKEN.
HUMM....

"I heard snake tastes like chicken," said Freddy.

"Echh!" I said.

"In China, they eat snake all the time," said Freddy.

“If you were in China,” said Eric, “you could have snake on a stick, snake-aroni, shishkasnake, and a snake shake.”

“They would all be snake snacks,” I smiled.

HORSE WITH TINY LEGS →

CHAPTER 9
THE HORSE'S MOUTH

Being the anchor was weighing me down. So I went to the speech teacher, Mrs. Mumbles, for exercises to improve my diction.

"Well, Hubie, Demosthenes, a famous Greek orator, practiced speaking with pebbles in his mouth," said Mrs. Mumbles.

"Did he ever swallow any?" I asked.

"I don't think so," said Mrs. Mumbles.

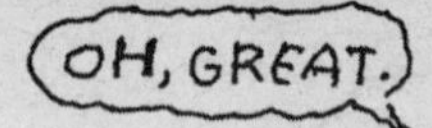

"Do you have any other tips?" I asked.

"There are jaw-stretching exercises," said Mrs. Mumbles. "Open your mouth as wide as possible and move it around in circles."

I did it.

"Good," said Mrs. Mumbles. "Now practice that as much as possible."

CHAPTER 10
BIG MOUTH

I practiced in class.

"Are you all right, Hubie?" asked Mrs. Green.

I practiced on the school bus.
"Are you all right?" asked Eric.

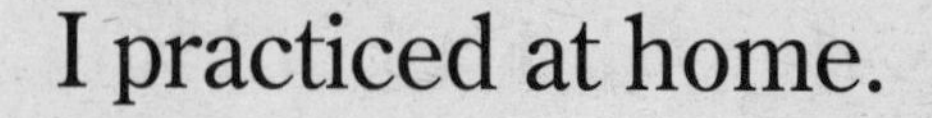

I practiced at home.

“Are you all right?” asked Mom.

“I-I-I-I AAAM FIIIINE,” I answered. “I’m in the home streeeeeeetch.”

I DON'T THINK MY MOUTH WILL CLOSE.
I CAN'T KEEP MY MOUTH OPEN ANY LONGER.

CHAPTER 11
ANCHORS AWAY

The day of the newscast finally arrived. I had to get up very early because Phil came on TV at 7:25 a.m.

Phil took his time as everyone stood around a little hole waiting for him to come out.

"Maybe he won't come out at all," I said, watching the TV.

"They may have to pull him out," said Mom.

"Maybe he has stage fright," I said.

"Maybe he forgot his lines," said Mom.

I was about to go have breakfast when a little nose poked out of the hole, then teeth, then ears, then a little fat body, then a tiny tail.

It was Punxsutawney Phil himself. He looked around, wiggled his nose, and went back in the hole.

All the officials looked at one another and wiggled their noses.

I looked at Mom and Mom looked at me. "I guess spring is in the air," I smiled.

CHAPTER 12
ON THE AIR

"Hello, kids, this is Hubie Cool with the news. Our headline this morning is that Groundhog Day got off with a little wiggle. Punxsutawney Phil forecast that spring will be here before you *nose* it. Now here's Freddy with the cafeteria menu."

ANCHOR

"Today we're having fish sticks, French fries, and Pepto-Bismol . . . only kidding. Luckily, we're not having the meat loaf monster."

"Now here's Derek with sports."

"In basketball, the fourth grade squeaked by the third grade, 107 to 6. The third grade is asking for a rematch."

"Now here's Penny with the society report."

"Doris is planning on giving Hubie a Valentine's Day card that says, 'I love you.'"

"Thank you," I said, blushing. "If we all stand up, Doris will give us her pledge . . . uh, the pledge . . . to our nation."

Doris put her hand on her heart and looked at me the whole time.

"Now last, but not least," I said, a little flustered. "Here's Eric with a knock-knock joke."

"Knock-Knock," said Eric.

"Who's there?" I asked.

"Phil," declared Eric.

"Phil who?" I asked.

"I've had my *Phil* of Groundhog Day," laughed Eric.

"Me too, and that wraps it up for the morning news this February second," I said.

PRINCIPAL'S OFFICE
HUBIE, GOOD MORNING AMERICA IS ON THE PHONE, AND I HAVE MESSAGES FROM NBC, CBS, AND ABC NEWS.
NO THANKS, I JUST WANT TO BE A KID.

CHAPTER 13
HEART TO HEART

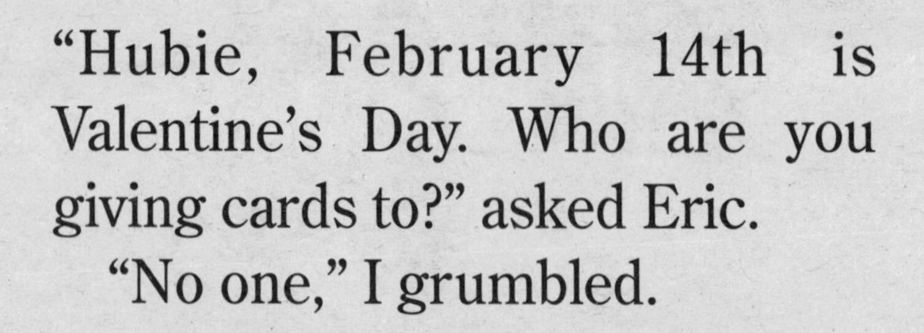

"Hubie, February 14th is Valentine's Day. Who are you giving cards to?" asked Eric.

"No one," I grumbled.

"No one?" said Eric. "You're going to break lots of hearts."

"Hum*heart*," I said. "If there's one holiday even more silly than Groundhog Day . . . it's Valentine's Day, and they both come in February."

"At least you get them over with early for the rest of the year," said Eric.

"You can say that again," I sighed.

"At least you get them over with early for the rest of the year," smiled Eric.

GROUNDHOG FACTS
1 ALSO KNOWN AS WOODCHUCKS OR WHISTLE-PIGS.
2 WEIGH 13 POUNDS AND 20 INCHES LONG.
3 THEY HIBERNATE FROM OCTOBER TO MARCH.
4 EAT GRASSES, BERRIES, VEGETABLES, TREE BARK, GRASSHOPPERS, INSECTS, AND SNAILS.
5 CAN SWIM AND ARE EXCELLENT TREE CLIMBERS.
6 A BABY GROUNDHOG IS CALLED A KIT OR CUB.
7 THEY DIG AND LIVE IN THEIR BURROWS, WHICH CAN BE 5 FEET BELOW GROUND.
8 GROUNDHOGS ARE RELATED TO SQUIRRELS.